This igloo book belongs to

....

igloobooks

Published in 2013
by Igloo Books Ltd
Cottage Farm
Sywell
NN6 0BJ
www.igloobooks.com

FIR003 0513
2 4 6 8 10 9 7 5 3 1
ISBN 978-1-78197-468-1

Illustrated by Marina Le Ray

Printed and manufactured in China

The Wheels on the Bus

igloobooks

The wheels on the bus go round and round,
round and round, round and round.
The wheels on the bus go round and round, all through the town.

BUS STOP

A B C

The animals on the bus get on and off, on and off, on and off.
The animals on the bus get on and off, all through the town.

The money on the bus goes jingle, jangle, jingle,
jingle, jangle, jingle, jingle, jangle, jingle.
The money on the bus goes jingle, jangle, jingle, all through the town.

The driver on the bus goes, "Move on back,
move on back, move on back."
The driver on the bus goes, "Move on back," all through the town.

The bell on the bus goes ding, ding, ding,
ding, ding, ding, ding, ding, ding.
The bell on the bus goes ding, ding, ding, all through the town.

The monkeys on the bus go oo-oo-oo, oo-oo-oo, oo-oo-oo.
The monkeys on the bus go oo-oo-oo, all through the town.

The motor on the bus goes vroom, vroom, vroom,
vroom, vroom, vroom, vroom, vroom, vroom.
The motor on the bus goes vroom, vroom, vroom, all through the town.

The horn on the bus goes beep, beep, beep,
beep, beep, beep, beep, beep, beep.
The horn on the bus goes beep, beep, beep, all through the town.

The mother hippos go chatter, chatter, chatter,
chatter, chatter, chatter, chatter, chatter, chatter.
The mother hippos go chatter, chatter, chatter, all through the town.

The daddy elephants go nod, nod, nod, nod, nod, nod, nod, nod, nod.
The daddy elephants go nod, nod, nod, all through the town.

The wipers on the bus go swish, swish, swish,
swish, swish, swish, swish, swish, swish.
The wipers on the bus go swish, swish, swish, all through the town.

The puddles on the road go splash, splash, splash,
splash, splash, splash, splash, splash, splash.
The puddles on the road go splash, splash, splash, all through the town.

The baby lion cubs go, "Wah, wah, wah, wah, wah, wah, wah, wah, wah."
The baby lion cubs go, "Wah, wah, wah," all through the town.

The little tiger tots go giggle, giggle, giggle,
giggle, giggle, giggle, giggle, giggle, giggle.
The little tiger tots go giggle, giggle, giggle, all through the town.

The traffic lights outside go stop, wait, go,
stop, wait, go, stop, wait, go.
The traffic lights outside go stop, wait, go, all through the town.

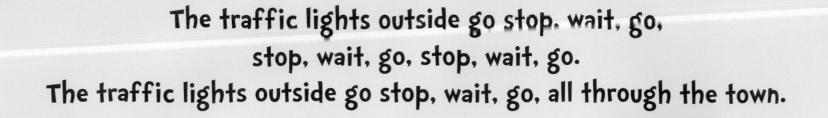

The signals on the bus go blink, blink, blink,
blink, blink, blink, blink, blink, blink.
The signals on the bus go blink, blink, blink, all through the town.

A B C

The grandpa gorillas go snore, snore, snore,
snore, snore, snore, snore, snore, snore.
The grandpa gorillas go snore, snore, snore, all through the town.

The grandma crocodiles go, shh, shh, shh,
shh, shh, shh, shh, shh, shh.
The grandma crocodiles go, shh, shh, shh, all through the town.

The bus goes round town until the sun goes down,
the sun goes down, the sun goes down.
The bus goes round town until the sun goes down, all through the town.

The animals on the bus go, "Here's my stop!
Here's my stop! Here's my stop!"
The animals on the bus go, "Here's my stop!" all through the town.

All through the town.